A LITTLE CRITTER® COLLECTION

FEELINGS AND MANNERS

BY MERCER MAYER

CHILDREN'S BOOK-OF-THE-MONTH CLUB
NEW YORK

FEELINGS AND MANNERS
A LITTLE CRITTER® COLLECTION

ALL BY MYSELF

BY MERCER MAYER

I can get out of bed
all by myself.

I can button
my overalls.

I can brush my fur.

I can put on my socks…

and tie my shoes.

I can pour some juice
for my little sister…

and help her eat breakfast.

I can pull a duck for her.

I can drive my truck.

I can ride my bike.

I can give a drink
to my bear.

I can kick my ball...

and roll on the ground.

I can pound with
my hammer.

I can sail my boat.

I can look after
my little sister.

I can help Dad
trim a bush…

or ice a cake for Mom.

I can look at a
book and find
a mouse.

I can color a picture.

I can put my toys away...

and get into my pajamas.

I can brush my teeth.

I can put myself to bed...

but I can't go to sleep
without a story.

Good night.

I WAS SO MAD

BY
MERCER MAYER

I wanted to keep some frogs in the bathtub but Mom wouldn't let me.

I was so mad.

I wanted to play
with my little sister's
dollhouse but Dad
wouldn't let me.

I was so mad.

I wanted to play hide-and-seek in the clean sheets but Grandma said, "No, you can't."

I was just so mad.

I wanted to water the garden
but Grandpa said,
"No, you can't."

So I decided to decorate the house but Grandpa said, "No, you can't do that, either."

Was I ever mad.

Dad said, "Why don't you play in the sandbox?"

I didn't want to do that.

Mom said, "Why don't you play on the slide?"

I didn't want to do that, either.
I was too mad.

I wanted to practice my juggling show, instead.

But Mom said, "No, you can't."

I wanted to tickle the goldfish but Mom said, "Leave the goldfish alone."

"You won't let me do anything I want to do," I said. "I guess I'll run away."

That's how mad I was.

So I packed my wagon
with my favorite toys.

And I packed a bag of cookies to eat on the way.

Then I walked out the front door.
But my friends were going to the
park to play ball.
"Can you come, too?" they asked.

And Mom said I could.

I'll run away tomorrow if I'm still so mad.

ME TOO!

BY MERCER MAYER

For Zeb
with love

When my little sister saw me riding my skateboard, she said...

Me too!

Then I had to help her ride.

I had a paper airplane
that I made myself.
But my little sister
saw it and said…

Me too!

Then she threw it
in a tree.

I went hiking with my friends and my little sister said, "Me too!"

Guess what my little sister said.

I went skating on the pond.
My little sister said, "Me too!"
She doesn't know how to skate,
so I had to hold her up.

There was one last piece of cake.
My little sister said…

I had to cut it in half,
even though I saw it first.

When I went fishing
she said, "Me too!"
Then she caught
the biggest fish.

I went to my secret tree house. My little sister said...

Me too!

Mom said I had to help her up.

Today my little sister
had a candy cane of
her very own.

Guess what my little sister said.

I JUST FORGOT

BY
MERCER MAYER

For Benjamin

Sometimes I remember, and
sometimes I just forget.

This morning I remembered to brush my teeth,
but I forgot to make my bed.

I put my dishes in the sink after breakfast,
but I forgot to put the milk away.

I almost forgot to feed the puppy, but he reminded me.

Grrrr

I didn't forget to water the plants. They looked fine to me.

I didn't forget to feed the goldfish.
He just didn't look hungry. I'll
do it now, Mom.

I got ready for school.
I even got to the school bus on time.

But I forgot my lunch box.

Mom brought it to school for me.
Thanks, Mom.

After school, I went outside to play in the rain.
I remembered to put on my rain slicker.

But I forgot my rubber boots.

When I came inside for a snack, I didn't forget to take my boots off. I left them on because I was going right back outside.

I had cookies and milk.

I was just going to eat three cookies, but
I forgot to count them.

I didn't forget to shut the refrigerator door, though.
I just wasn't finished eating yet.

When Dad came home from work, I was supposed to get his paper. I didn't forget—the puppy got it first.

I know it's time for bed. I didn't forget.

Of course I'll remember to pick up my toys when
I'm finished playing with them.

I took my bath and remembered to wash behind my ears.

I didn't use soap, but I didn't forget to. I just don't like soap.

I guess I did forget to pick up my toys.

Did I forget to turn off the tub, too?

But there is one thing I never forget.

I always remember to have Mom
read me a bedtime story. And I always remember
to kiss her good night.

I'M SORRY

BY GINA AND
MERCER MAYER

Whenever I do something wrong,
I just say, "I'm sorry."

I knocked my sister off her bicycle by accident.
I said, "I'm sorry."

I left my sister's jump rope at the park.
I said, "I'm sorry."
We had to walk all the way back to get it.

I used my brother's blanket for my Super Critter cape. It got dirty when I was playing outside. I said, "I'm sorry."

When I was playing hide-and-seek with my sister, I got
tangled in the curtain and pulled it down. I said, "I'm sorry."

When I was trying to reach my favorite book, I knocked all the other books down. I said, "I'm sorry."

Mom helped me put them all back.

Mom said, "The baby is napping, so please play quietly."

I forgot to play quietly. I woke the baby.

I said, "I'm sorry."
Mom said, "Go play
outside."

I didn't know the baby's bedroom window
was open. "I'm sorry, Mom," I said.

When I was playing football, I got tackled in Mom's garden. I said, "Sorry!"

Mom and Dad asked me to close my bedroom window
when it rained, but I forgot. I said, "I'm sorry."

I didn't empty my pockets before Mom washed my pants. I said, "I'm sorry."

Mom said, "That's what you said last time."

I really wasn't sorry that I forgot to clean my room. I hate to do that.

But I really was sorry
when I stepped in a
mud puddle with
my new shoes . . .

and that I didn't
wash my hands
before I picked up
the baby's bunny.

But I was especially sorry
that I left the top off my ant farm.

At dinner, Dad put some broccoli on my plate. I said, "I'm sorry, I don't like broccoli."

Dad said, "I'm sorry, you have to eat some anyway."

I was kind of messy when I was taking a bath. I said, "I'm sorry."
Dad made me clean up the bathroom.

After I took apart my sister's dollhouse, I couldn't put it back together. I said I was sorry. My sister called Mom.

While Mom fixed the dollhouse, I was supposed to watch my little brother. Oops!

I said, "I'm sorry, Mom."
Mom said, "Sometimes saying
'I'm sorry' just isn't good enough."

I didn't know that.

If saying "I'm sorry" isn't good enough,
I guess I'll just have to be more careful.

JUST A BULLY

BY GINA AND MERCER MAYER

*For Zeb, Ben,
and Arden*

Mom and Dad told Little Sister and me to always stick up for each other.

One day a bigger kid was picking on
my little sister at the playground.

That's when it all started.
Because that kid started to pick on me.

On the school bus he would sit behind me and pull my fur or steal my hat and not give it back.

He would try to trip me when I walked down the hall.

In the auditorium he would shoot me with rubber bands.

He would call me
names and stick out
his tongue at me.

I told the teacher that the bully was picking on me. She said she would take care of it. But after she talked to him it got even worse.

The next day I didn't want to go
to school, so I pretended I was sick.

I think Mom knew I was pretending,
but she let me stay home anyway.

My little sister came in my room after school and said, "Don't let that bully get to you. Just give him a punch."

But I was too scared to punch him
because I might get beat up.

On school project day the bully took my project away
from me. I asked for it back, but he just laughed at me.

So I tried to pull it out of his hands.
He wouldn't let go and my project broke.
"I'll get you later," he said.

I was nervous all day. Finally the bell rang. Sure enough, he was waiting for me by the bus. I was real scared.

I tried to walk by him, but he pushed me.
"Just leave me alone!" I said.

He said, "You're not going anywhere,"
and pushed me real hard.

So I took a deep breath and started swinging.
I think he hit me a lot more than I hit him.

When a teacher broke it up, we got a good
scolding. Then we had to get on the bus.

My legs were so shaky that I could barely
walk. All the kids gave me five.

As the bully walked to the back of the bus, my little sister was waiting. She yelled, "Hey, fathead! Leave my big brother alone!" Then she shoved him real hard.

The bully didn't do anything to my little sister.
He didn't dare. He just walked to the front of the
bus and sat down.

There is one thing for sure. My little sister is tough.
That bully better not mess with me or her ever again.